EXPLORING THEATER

Singing in Theater

Ruth Bjorklund

New York

Published in 2018 by Cavendish Square Publishing, LLC
243 5th Avenue, Suite 136, New York, NY 10016

Copyright © 2018 by Cavendish Square Publishing, LLC

First Edition

No part of this publication may be reproduced, stored in a retrieval system, or transmitted in any form or by any means—electronic, mechanical, photocopying, recording, or otherwise—without the prior permission of the copyright owner. Request for permission should be addressed to Permissions, Cavendish Square Publishing, 243 5th Avenue, Suite 136, New York, NY 10016. Tel (877) 980-4450; fax (877) 980-4454.

Website: cavendishsq.com

This publication represents the opinions and views of the author based on his or her personal experience, knowledge, and research. The information in this book serves as a general guide only. The author and publisher have used their best efforts in preparing this book and disclaim liability rising directly or indirectly from the use and application of this book.

All websites were available and accurate when this book was sent to press.

Library of Congress Cataloging-in-Publication Data

Names: Bjorklund, Ruth.
Title: Singing in theater / Ruth Bjorklund.
Description: New York : Cavendish Square, 2018. | Series: Exploring theater | Includes index. | Audience: Grades 7-12.
Identifiers: ISBN 9781502630070 (library bound) | ISBN 9781502634290 (pbk.) | ISBN 9781502630087 (ebook)
Subjects: LCSH: Singing--Juvenile literature. | Theater--Juvenile literature.
Classification: LCC PN2037.B54 2018 | DDC 792--dc23

Editorial Director: David McNamara
Editor: Fletcher Doyle
Copy Editor: Nathan Heidelberger
Associate Art Director: Amy Greenan
Designer: Jessica Nevins
Production Coordinator: Karol Szymczuk
Photo Research: J8 Media

The photographs in this book are used by permission and through the courtesy of: Cover Wildbild/AFP/Getty Images; p. 4, 56 Robbie Jack/Corbis via Getty Images; p. 9 Stray Cat/E+/Getty Images; p. 11, 51 Hill Street Studios/Blend Images/Getty Images; p. 14 XiXinXing/iStock/Thinkstock.com; p. 17 Gregory Rec/Portland Press Herald/Getty Images; p. 20 Clu/iStockphoto.com; p. 24 Zuma Press/Alamy Stock Photo; p. 26 Carol Rosegg/Broadway Across America/Getty Images; p. 28 Cindy Ord/Getty Images; p. 31 Groovepup/Wikimedia Commons/File:Actress Ella Thomas Headsho.jpg/CC BY SA 3.0; p. 35, 60 PA Images/Alamy Stock Photo; p. 38 Jupiter Images/Photo Library/Getty Images; p. 40 Fairfax Media via Getty Images; p. 43 Jeffrey Greenberg/UIG/Getty Images; p. 46 Yuri Shevtsov/Shutterstock.com; p. 52 AP Images; p. 59, 74 Walter McBride/Corbis/Getty Images; p. 63 Matthew Peyton/Getty Images for Stellar Productions; p. 64 Lisa Maree Williams/Getty Images; p. 69 Dreet Production/Getty Images; p. 71 VisitBritain/Eric Nathan/Getty Images; p. 78 S. Bukley/Shutterstock.com; p. 80 Carlos Chavez/Los Angeles Times/Getty Images; p. 82 Brian Ach/Getty Images; p. 86 Hero Images/Getty Images.

Printed in the United States of America

CONTENTS

Chapter 1:	Something's Coming	5
Chapter 2:	Great Teams	16
Chapter 3:	The Music in You	29
Chapter 4:	High Hopes	61
Chapter 5:	What Comes Next	75

Glossary	88
For More Information	91
Index	94
About the Author	96

Two singers perform their roles as star-crossed lovers Tony and Maria in the balcony scene from *West Side Story*.

CHAPTER ONE

Something's Coming

West Side Story is a Broadway musical by Steven Sondheim and Leonard Bernstein, two of the most acclaimed composers and lyricists of all time. Their music has inspired singers for decades. For most singers, singing is a part of each and every day. Whether in the car, in the shower, cleaning the house, or making lunch, people who enjoy singing look for every opportunity to break into song. Many sing simply for fun, but others hope their talent and love of singing might result in a career onstage and under the lights. Being a performer in musical theater is one of the most rewarding, exciting, and challenging careers imaginable.

Talent and Beyond

Most singers first become enamored of musical theater by acting in high school musicals or community theater. Students often get their first taste of performing in a school choir. Even if you are inclined toward solo performing, joining the school choir is something you should do. In the school choir, you will get professional guidance from your director.

In the choir, you will learn warm-up exercises to prepare you to sing correctly. You will be instructed in posture, breathing, and other techniques that will reduce strain on your vocal cords and improve your tone and **pitch**. Also, you will learn how to blend your voice with others, a valuable skill should you decide to pursue a career in musical theater.

If you love to sing, can really sing, and want to see how far in the world you can go, there is a lot to consider. But a serious career in musical theater is far from the fun and short-lived excitement of performing for classmates, friends, and family. A musical theater career demands considerable amounts of training and practice. It is a complex and sometimes painful career, but one with many thrilling rewards.

First, above all, a person hoping to sing and be a part of musical theater must have natural talent. However, having raw talent is not the only factor, and many fail to recognize that right away. Anyone wanting to make it professionally needs to look at what goes into a successful onstage career. A beautiful or distinctive voice opens the door, but persistence, a work ethic, and good training and support are behind the people who ace the **auditions** and get the roles.

The Voice

Many people talk about raw, or natural, talent. While it no doubt is a prerequisite, you still need to develop your voice and get a feel for what your special forte might be. Singing is more than having a good voice. Singers who start off singing very young will naturally learn many important skills on their own. They will develop vocal strength and an ear for harmony and melody. But becoming a singer, a professional singer, requires study and practice.

A singer needs to accept that a beautiful or stirring voice on its own will not carry him or her in the long run, without help and training. A young person who loves singing with a passion, such as one who stars in every grade school and high school production, can easily damage or strain his or her voice over time, without guidance. That first guidance will come from your school's choir director. However, the director will have many students to guide and won't be able to give you the attention you may need. So, anyone who wants to pursue a singing career should be willing to seek out professional help, whether by taking classes or training with a voice or singing coach. This is no different than someone in the school band taking private lessons after school.

There are several ways to get help training your voice. At the most basic, it will come from the teachers who run the theater department at a high school. A guidance counselor can also help get you accepted into a community college music class. There are summer camps for the performing arts, and often scholarships are available. Check out classifieds for people who advertise as private music, singing, or voice instructors.

Community theater is also a possibility. Granted, there are few singing roles and rarely any major singing roles in community theater for a young person. However, a good audition may get you noticed and land you a place in the chorus. That is the place where most people get their first taste of performing in musical theater.

Being a Voice Student

When you decide to hire a singing or vocal coach, you have a duty to yourself to get the most benefit possible from the experience. Before working with a coach, it is important to set up an interview. The two of you must be able to work together. The coach will want to hear you sing, and it is important to sing something that shows off your voice and expresses your style, whether jazz, pop, rock, Disney, standards, or operetta. Pay attention to what the vocal or singing coach has to say about your voice. You are more likely to benefit from someone who can right away point out a few things to focus on to improve your voice.

A good singing or vocal coach can help you be more expressive in your vocal delivery. The coach will help you extend your **vocal range** incrementally so that you do not strain yourself. A good vocal coach will be able to assess your strengths and weaknesses. He or she will provide you with exercises for facial muscles, throat, tongue, teeth, vocal cords, posture, and breathing. The coach will help you develop pitch, tone, fullness, and volume. Having the ability to sing comfortably with a variety of styles and tones will broaden your chances of getting into a good college or conservatory or getting a job. If you live in a large city, you will likely find singing or vocal coaches who specialize in your preferred style, or genre.

In the interview, it would be very advantageous for you to discuss who the coach knows in the

Taking lessons from a vocal coach can develop a singer's range, delivery, and technique.

business, such as agents, producers, directors, and/or **choreographers.** Theater is a very social profession, and who you know and who you may have the opportunity to meet will help further your career. Also in the interview, it will be important to discuss your goals. The coach should suggest ways to achieve those goals while taking into account your personal schedule.

Getting Started

Where can you go to get started? Likely you have a busy school and personal schedule. You may even have a part-time job. None of that means you cannot start getting involved. It is important to seek out resources, such as books, movies, productions of live theater, and **cast recordings**. You might find going out for karaoke a helpful way to get used to singing onstage.

Get comfortable with musical theater. Attend performances. Many theaters offer "pay what you can" nights or give student discounts. Some theaters allow people to watch the final rehearsals. You may want to look for a job as an usher or backstage volunteer at a community theater. All of these things will look good on a résumé should you decide to pursue parts in musicals after leaving high school. Learn a variety of songs, rhythms, and the sounds instruments produce. Become familiar with popular musicals for school and community theater, such as *Beauty and the Beast, Seussical, Into the Woods, Little Shop of Horrors,* and *Grease.*

Learning How to Audition

Auditions are a job and an art form. They are more than just knowing a song and singing it well. Auditions require an enormous amount of concentration, research, and preparation. High school productions have fewer audition requirements than community, regional, college, and professional productions. However, there are many basics that apply. It is imperative that you study the character and be familiar with the plot and the music in the play. Know which parts sing songs in your vocal ranges. Do not overdress. Always be polite, and thank the casting director and the **accompanist**. If no

These students must schedule their school and home life in order to practice their singing and dancing routines after school.

accompanist is scheduled to attend, bring a recording to back up your singing.

Goal Setting and Planning

Once you have been bitten by the theater bug, you should start to define your goals. Will you be content with being in the drama program at school or with an

Something's Coming 11

occasional role in a community theater production? Do you want to study music, theater, and the performing arts in college or other theater programs? Do you want to pursue singing in musical theater as a professional career?

If you aspire to a professional career in musical theater, you will face a lot of planning and decisions. The idea or hope that you will be discovered randomly or that your raw talent will catapult you to fame and fortune is a myth. A career in musical theater requires serious planning skills. Plan to get the best training you possibly can. Research college programs, theater schools, and private instructors. Prepare a résumé. You may find that majoring in theater or music in college is as far as you need to go. Those subjects can also provide you with a great background for many other careers. The key to knowing how to plan is being able to read the signs that will guide you if, or when, you decide to change course. If you remain true to your original plan, you will rely on your planning skills to determine where you want to live and how you will support yourself. Do you want to try living in a big city? In a university town? A community with a thriving regional theater? Possibly you may decide to teach.

Get Physical

Every singer who hopes to be cast in a musical will need to know how to dance and move gracefully onstage. A typical casting notice for a musical will read either, "Dancer who can sing," "Singer who can dance," or "Actor who can sing and dance." What this means for a singing career in musical theater is the need for a variety of onstage skills. Most singing roles call for dancing or physically communicating to the audience your emotions. So, besides keeping your voice in shape, it is necessary to keep your body fit. Practice a variety of dance styles, just as you would practice a variety of singing styles. Be sure to schedule regular workout times and do exercises such as running, jumping, and swimming. It is also a very good idea to take a course in stage combat.

Of course, a lead-in to being physically fit is following a healthy lifestyle. A diet of fruits, vegetables, whole grains, and small portions of meat and fish is important. Avoid tobacco, and cut down on sugar, gluten, carbohydrates, and high-fat foods. Always have a healthy breakfast, and if you are running late for school, grab at least a piece of fruit, such as a banana or an apple, to eat on the way. This is crucial because without a good breakfast you can run out of energy during the day and lose concentration. If you are auditioning or rehearsing after school, it is critical that you maintain your strength and energy during the day.

Singing on a theater stage is more than a display of talent. Behind each note, each movement, is a person who has studied, practiced, and put in an amazing amount of effort. Performers in musical theater not only must be able to sing, they must also know how to act, dance, and move onstage. A person who sings, acts, and dances is known as a **triple threat**. Beyond singing lessons, successful singers

Taking classes in yoga, martial arts, or Zumba can improve a performer's balance and movement.

also need instruction and experience in a variety of theater arts.

Other Valuable Skills

Taking improvisation classes or workshops is useful and quite enjoyable. The training is especially useful in preventing you from being knocked off your guard in an audition. Body and movement classes, which could include tai chi, aikido, or yoga, are helpful in relaxing your body, improving your posture, and helping you move more gracefully across the stage. This can be of benefit when you are trying to maintain even breathing so you can hold a note for a long period while moving.

Organization Skills

Without organization skills, you will never get far in your career. Beginning as a student, you will need to keep track of a tight schedule of classes, private singing lessons, dance or yoga classes, and theater rehearsals. Once out of school, you will be doing much the same and likely working a job besides singing. A well-planned calendar is essential. Being late for auditions and practices, not to mention performances, is unacceptable.

As a professional singer, you must develop and keep a songbook of at least twenty-five pieces of music you know thoroughly. The songs should be of a variety of styles, such as jazz, show tunes, rock, country, and musical standards. You will also need to accompany your songbook with sheet music. In any professional audition, there will be an accompanist, usually a piano player, who will need the sheet music you provide. It is always a good idea to change songs in your songbook, to keep you and your auditions fresh.

CHAPTER TWO

Great Teams

As a singer and performer in musical theater, you will find yourself on many teams. It is very important to recognize your role in any given team and perform accordingly. You will be on a study team, an audition team, a practice team, a behind-the-scenes team, and a live stage production team. In some instances, it may be your role to be simply polite and conscientious. In other instances, however, you may be the one others rely on to carry the show.

The Voice Student

In whatever form your voice instruction comes, whether in a classroom or through private voice or singing lessons, you are responsible for paying attention, being organized, and arriving on time. It is your end of the bargain to practice and come to class prepared. You will be given exercises to train your body and your voice, and assignments to manipulate your mouth, control your breathing, and develop your tone, rhythm, and pitch. Of course, you will also

Many singers get their start performing in a school choir.

learn how to sing scales, notes, and songs. The voice or singing instructor is there to listen, correct how you sing, and teach you how to protect your voice and make it resonate. You must respectfully accept criticism and use it to your best advantage.

A voice coach provides you with guidance in determining the best material and style for you to practice. The coach will accompany you and teach you how to perform for auditions. A good vocal coach will help you communicate the meaning or emotion of your songs to your listeners, and show you how to engage your audience. Vocal coaches also help give you advice about overcoming your stage fright and show you how to be relaxed and natural looking when you sing. All voice instructors and vocal coaches are experienced singers who do not want to waste time teaching someone who is not taking their art seriously.

Great Teams 17

Banding Together

You are called in for an audition. It may seem as if everyone else in the waiting room is your competitor or your adversary. It is not wholly true. You as performers will see each other in the same lobbies and waiting rooms many, many times. You will more than likely work together many times. Coming together as a creative community is so important. Networking with other aspiring singers, dancers, and actors will advance your career in many ways. These personal connections will offer you advice and share information about other auditions and opportunities. You will also be there for each other to give much-needed moral support. No one knows better what you are going through than they do.

The Production Team

You have made the cut and have a role in a musical. You have a lot of work ahead of you. Before you begin, you will get acquainted with the creative team, the technical team, and the cast. You will work closely with some of the members of the production, and with some less so.

You will be introduced to the other cast members, as well as the director, stage manager, music director, accompanists, musicians, and choreographer. You may even work with the playwright and the composer. Later, as the show progresses, you will interact with the lighting and sound engineers, the set designer, stagehands, and the costume department.

The Creative Team and Performers

Your introduction to the play will come from the director. You will have been given the script and the sheet music to study. Then you and the cast (not always the full cast) will have your first meetings to discuss the director's vision. Although many musical theater productions are not original works, every director takes a fresh look. In the early meetings, the director will discuss his or her interpretation of the characters, including their emotions, mood, and temperament. The director will also discuss the relationship between characters, as well as the context, setting, time period, and plot. He or she will tell the cast where the music, songs, and dances will appear, as well as how they will be expressed.

In larger productions, there is also a music director. He or she will lead the music rehearsals for the principal singers, the chorus, accompanists, and the musicians. The music director will teach the cast the show's music—songs, tempo, and rhythm. He or she will help you understand how the music and your voice will create mood, dramatic tension, and setting. The music director coordinates his or her needs and expectations with those of the director and the choreographer.

Larger shows often require the talents of a choreographer. This is the person responsible for designing the dance routines and teaching them to the cast. Most singers will take instruction from a

A lead singer practices along with her chorus and accompanist during an early reheasal.

choreographer, as many singing roles require some dancing. For singers cast in a chorus, there is nearly always dancing involved. If a singer does not have to dance, he or she still requires direction on where and how to move about the stage. The director, the stage manager, and/or the choreographer will work with performers to position them on the stage.

The director and choreographer will determine the movements of the actors and singers. Performers keep notes on their assignments and the stage manager (or in the case of a small production, the director) keeps the master book, called the **prompt**

book. The stage manager writes down those movements in the prompt book and ensures that cast members follow them onstage. He or she will give directions to the actors and singers, especially during the early rehearsals. Some common stage directions are "stage right," "downstage left," "up center," "cross," and "enter."

The best relationship for you as a performer in musical theater is collaboration. Especially if you are a principal in the production, the directors and managers may appreciate your feedback. It is always fortunate when comments and questions are accepted. But be certain to keep your comments and suggestions to a minimum. Additionally, minor characters and chorus members should refrain from voicing opinions unprompted. No matter how receptive the creative team is to your input, the directors have the final word.

Throughout rehearsals, you will work closely with the rehearsal pianist. The orchestra will have its own rehearsals with the conductor, who will have a copy of the script as well as the musical score. Once rehearsals get close to opening night, you will begin to work with the orchestra. This will give the members of the orchestra the time to learn the pacing of the play as well as the vocal interpretations of the music. Dance numbers will also have to be practiced with the full orchestra so everybody can be in sync. When the rehearsals near the final stages, you will find yourself working with other members of the creative team—the sound and lighting engineers, costume designer and wardrobe department, stagehands, and the technical department.

Coordinating the Nuts and Bolts

Besides learning the musical and creative part of your performance, you will also need to be aware of some technical issues. A sound engineer may explain to you how the acoustics work on the stage and in the theater and help you adjust your volume most effectively. Set materials such as draperies or upholstered furniture will absorb sound and diminish your voice. Conversely, a stark set may distort your voice. You will be supplied with microphones. The sound engineer will ensure your voice projects to the entire theater while the music director will tell you how to make your voice blend in volume and in harmony with other singers. While the principal singer or singers dominate a song, the chorus is heard at varying levels. But sometimes the chorus takes over a portion of the song, and microphones need to pick up what the music director has intended.

The lighting engineer will explain to you how his or her lighting plan will highlight your performance. If you are a principal in the production, the lighting will accentuate the mood of your songs. If you are in the chorus, you will not generally be featured in the lighting scheme. However, many live theater performers apply their own makeup. Knowing how the lighting will affect your stage appearance is a big help in deciding how to do your makeup.

Singers also work with costume designers who are tasked with visually interpreting your character's image or role. In fittings with the costume designer, it is important to let him or her know if the bodice or neck of the shirt, dress, or blouse prevents you from breathing correctly. Singers with dancing roles need to be sure their costumes are designed and fitted to allow adequate freedom of movement. Usually, and most productively, the costume designer or wardrobe manager will supply you with the shoes you will wear well in advance of the rest of the costume so that you may practice with them. Singers, and especially dancers, need to get their balance and foundation established throughout the rehearsal period. Costume designers should also supply you early with any unusual or awkward costume pieces, such as a hoop skirt, a pair of wings, or a large, floppy hat. They also must make sure the costume and any accessories do not interfere with the microphone or create any noises that might be picked up by the microphone and broadcast to the audience.

Rehearsals

Up until opening night, you will not experience any greater sense of teamwork than during rehearsals. Rehearsals follow a strict schedule, and to be fair to everyone in the production, you need to clear your own personal schedule and make yourself available. You will not be responsible for appearing each time there is a rehearsal; some rehearsals are for specific characters. However, even when you are called for rehearsal, you may find that the director needs more time to focus on another part of the play. In that case,

A director makes a point with his cast during a break in a full-dress rehearsal.

you may be backstage the entire time. That does not mean you can leave. While some cast members bring work or reading with them, it is really better to spend your time watching the rehearsal and taking notes.

Rehearsals usually begin with the cast and director. Everyone brings a copy of the script and reads through it the first time together. Often singers will have some speaking parts. If you do not have a speaking role, the read-through is nonetheless vital. You will get a sense of the characters in the play, and of how the songs and musical numbers enhance the script. The actors with speaking roles also need

24 Singing in Theater

to be familiar with the songs. The director or music director will perform the music with an accompanist for the entire cast. Hearing the music in the earliest stages helps everyone feel connected and excited about the play. In high schools, music rooms can be turned into rehearsal spaces after school. Chorus numbers can be perfected before the group even gets onstage, and leads can learn the nuances of their parts without anybody watching.

The director will publish a rehearsal schedule. Full cast rehearsals do not occur until near the end of the rehearsal period. According to a set schedule, you will be called for rehearsals with the director, music director, choreographer, the accompanists, orchestra, other singers, and dancers. Sometimes only the principals, or leads, will have singing rehearsals, and sometimes only the musicians or dancers will be called to rehearsal. Depending on your role, you could find yourself attending all the rehearsals. During the course of the rehearsal period, cast members give each other feedback and encouragement. Throughout the rehearsal period, close friendships often form.

A Chorus Line

In a musical production, there is no greater example of teamwork than the chorus. In the chorus, every voice is different, but each voice is necessary to create the highest quality of sound. Singers in a chorus are often dancers as well. Dancing in a chorus requires learning the dance numbers and being able to perform without thinking. Not only will you need to be aware of what the rest of the chorus is doing, but you

A touring company performs *Rent* during the play's twentieth anniversary.

should look out for one another. Should you make a misstep, if you come in too early or too late, or if you hit the wrong note, your chorus colleagues will be there to cover for you. Musicals are centered around the main characters and principal singers. However, the chorus often ties the whole production together. Many great musicals went on to higher levels of fame because of well-sung, well-danced, and noteworthy chorus numbers. Some award-winning shows known

for their chorus numbers include *Les Misérables, A Chorus Line, Urinetown, Rent, West Side Story,* and *Wicked.*

Family

In a musical theater production, people work closely together, usually with long hours and often under strain. They are truly dependent on one another. Given the intensity of the relationships, most everyone in a musical production says they feel a part of a substitute family. And while there are people with more responsibilities and more time onstage, without everyone's efforts and contributions, there would be no play and no performance.

A long line of hopefuls wait to audition in response to an open casting call.

CHAPTER THREE
The Music in You

Once you decide you want to sing in musical theater, your first step is the audition. Audition times will be posted at your school in a number of places. If you are new to a school or are just considering trying out for the play, ask the choir director when auditions will be held. It will let that person know you are interested.

For auditions outside of school, there are several print newsletters and magazines that list casting calls and websites, such as Backstage.com and Actor's Access. The casting calls will tell you the date, time, and location of the auditions. The notice will include information about the character's personality, the type of musical, the vocal range required, the plot, the venue, and the intended run. The notice may also indicate if there are specific characteristics wanted, such as age range, body type, dance talent, ethnicity, and/or gender. You will need to submit a résumé and **headshot** to the casting director. Professional headshots can be expensive, so don't have them taken unless you are serious about the theater. However, they are necessary and can get you in the door if the director is searching for a specific physical type.

Many of your first auditions will be responses to open casting calls. An open casting call is a published notice for a role or roles open to anyone who would like to try out. These are rarely for principal roles, and often they are for the chorus. An open casting call can be very crowded and very stressful. At one recent open casting call, lines formed around the theater, and the casting director was deluged with more than nine hundred hopeful actors, singers, and dancers. But as your career progresses, you will likely submit your credentials to the casting department, and an agent will find and schedule auditions for you. But whether it is your first or your one hundredth audition, you have a great deal of preparation to do.

Résumé and Headshot

Start keeping track of all you do as soon as you realize that you love singing and want to try to do it after getting out of high school. Get onstage as often as possible, and write down what you did so you will have a record when it comes time to prepare a résumé.

Before any community theater or professional audition, you will need to prepare a résumé and have a professional portrait taken. This is known as a headshot. You may submit your credentials online to professional databases, but you will also turn hard copies of those credentials in to the audition director's assistant. You ought to bring several copies in case you need to pass them to other casting directors, such as the music director or choreographer.

Your résumé should take up only one page. It should deliver all the important information about you

Actress Ella Thomas uses this headshot to promote the look that got her started on network television.

within the ten-second glance of an audition or casting director. This is often called the "Ten-Second Rule."

Choosing Your Song

Well in advance of any audition, you will have developed a cover book, a binder with fifteen to twenty-five songs that you are prepared to sing at an

The Music in You 31

audition. The binder includes lyrics and sheet music for eight-, sixteen-, or thirty-two-bar selections from those songs.

Decide what you plan to sing far enough in advance so that you can practice, but not so much in advance that it seems stale and no longer fresh to you. The process of choosing a song might also give you a chance to learn new songs, which can never hurt. As for your song choice, stay away from classic songs. Audition and casting directors are exhausted from hearing featured songs from major hits, such as *Phantom of the Opera, Chicago, The Wizard of Oz, Les Misérables,* or anything Disney. On the other hand, it will be important to sing something catchy and somewhat familiar.

You will likely have an accompanist at the audition, and you must prepare your music for him or her. Some people hand the accompanist their cover book, but many believe that it is more respectful to print out a copy of the sheet music to hand to the accompanist. You should not count on him or her knowing your song choice, so do not select a piece that is particularly difficult to sight-read. Know in advance, as best you can, how many bars the audition director will want to hear. If you do not know in advance, be prepared to sing the full song, or otherwise an eight-, sixteen-, or thirty-two-bar portion of your song. Clearly mark those selections, preferably in red, for the accompanist.

Decide on a song that suits both you and the production. If the play has a jazz theme, choose something appropriate but within your strongest vocal range. If the musical is lighthearted, go with an up-tempo piece. If the play is very dramatic, choose a slower song, but not so slow that you cannot capture attention.

You Are What You Sing

One thing to keep in mind when choosing a role to audition for is that your voice, or vocal range, will most often determine the kinds of roles you receive. Although this is a traditional rule, times are changing, and roles are expanding into a variety of vocal types. However, it is still more common that a singer's vocal range determines the type of character he or she will play.

The highest female voice range is a **soprano**. Sopranos are often cast as the female romantic lead. If she is cast in the chorus, she is often a soloist. Rapunzel and Cinderella from *Into the Woods* are soprano roles.

The most common vocal range for women is **mezzo-soprano**. Most mezzo-sopranos can **belt** and are often leads in pop/rock musicals. In other types of musicals, a mezzo-soprano often sings a supporting role—best friend or rival—such as the Baker's Wife in *Into the Woods* or Cosette in *Les Misérables*.

Alto, also called contralto, is the lowest female vocal range. There are many types of roles for altos, especially in rock musicals, such as Rose in *Dogfight*.

Tenors have the highest male vocal range. (Countertenor is actually the highest, but it is rarely heard or sung anymore. If a young boy sings in a high vocal register, his voice is called a boy soprano). Tenors, like sopranos, are cast as the romantic leads and as the "good guys," such as Angel in *Rent*, Tony in *West Side Story*, and Elder Price in *The Book of Mormon*.

Baritone is the most common vocal range for men. Baritones can be cast in a variety of roles: as leading men, villains, character roles, and secondary leads. As there are so many baritones, there are also baritone subtypes. Villains and leads tend to be dramatic baritones who can belt. Baritones singing as character roles are generally more lighthearted, and their vocal range is called comic baritone. Lighter roles or "everyday" guys usually sing a type of baritone called lyric baritone. The roles of the King of Siam in *The King and I* and Henry Higgins in *My Fair Lady* are baritones.

Men with a **bass** (lowest) vocal range are rare in musical theater, although not so in opera. In musical theater, basses are usually cast as villains or authority figures. An example is Judge Turpin in *Sweeney Todd*. He is both an authority figure and a villain.

What Are You Singing?

Another factor to consider in auditioning is that there are several types of musical theater songs. Some you will perform or prefer more than others. If you are lucky enough to make a career of singing, you may decide to specialize in only a certain type of musical. Some singers have chosen to specialize in just one musical or even just one character. However, if you are in high school, you will have to sing whatever music is in the selected show. Keep in mind that in high school, directors generally know what talent is available and match the show to the voices in the school. A director will never pick a show if there is a song no one in the school can sing.

A show ballad is a slow and melodic song with a rhythmic beat that is early in the play. It is usually a love song. Many songs of this type can be sung outside of the play and retain their meaning, such as "Tonight" from *West Side Story* or "Tomorrow" from *Annie*. These love songs can be among the most

This singer, in the role of Eva Peron, is performing her eleven o'clock number, "Don't Cry for Me, Argentina."

difficult in a show and don't even have to be sung by a lead character. If you prefer singing to acting, this might provide you with a perfect role in a musical. Examples are "Younger Than Springtime" from *South Pacific* and "On the Street Where You Live" from *My Fair Lady.*

A narrative ballad is also slow and melodic, but the lyrics reflect the play and help move the plot along. This type of song tells something about the character and usually describes loss of love, longing, or self-discovery, such as, "Somewhere That's Green" from *Little Shop of Horrors* or "The Wizard and I" from *Wicked.*

Some musicals have blues numbers, such as "Am I Blue?" from *Blues in the Night.* Others feature jazz, such as "Devil and the Deep Blue Sea" from *After Midnight.* There are rock songs, such as "Sincerely, Me" from *Dear Evan Hansen*; up-tempo ballads, such as "Stepping to the Bad Side" from *Dreamgirls*; and more recently, hip-hop numbers such as "Ten Duel Commandments" from *Hamilton.*

A dramatic show ballad often comes near the finale. It is the song that is the most rousing, and it usually resolves the plot. It requires a lot of passion and is difficult to sing. It is also known as the **"eleven o'clock number."** The meaning behind the phrase is that musicals traditionally began on Broadway at 8:45 p.m. By 11:00 p.m., the play was nearing its end. This was the time reserved for the star, sometimes backed up by the chorus, to deliver his or her showstopping performance. Examples would be "Memory" from *Cats* and "Don't Cry for Me, Argentina" from *Evita.*

At some point you may be singing the eleven o'clock number. Treasure the role and experience. It will be one you will never forget, and it could launch your career.

Musical Theater Genres

There are several genres of musical theater, and many today have reduced the number to four basic categories. You may prefer, and be better suited for, one genre over the others. Knowing your strengths can help guide you to the right auditions.

Legit is a type of musical that is associated with traditional musicals. Singers generally have classical voices and training, a balanced tone, and crisp articulation. Most legit musicals come from the "Golden Age of Broadway," such as *Guys and Dolls*, but there are also a few contemporary musicals in this genre, such as *A Gentleman's Guide to Love and Murder*.

Traditional musical theater is a genre that focuses on lyrics and crisp vocalization. The type of singing involved is called **belt**, or a chest-voice type of singing. *Cabaret* and *Chicago* are two musicals in this genre.

Contemporary musical theater blends pop and rock music with belt singing. The lyrics of songs in this genre drive the plot of the play. An example would be *Wicked*.

Pop/rock musical theater includes a variety of vocal styles including pop, rock, country, hip-hop, and rhythm and blues. Singing style is often featured more than the lyrics. Examples of this genre include *Rent* and *Next to Normal*.

When auditioning, it is important to dress casually and comfortably.

Appearances

Appearances are an essential part of the audition. Be neat. Wear something you are comfortable in. Know the role you are auditioning for, and use it to influence, but not dictate, what you wear to the audition. If the play is historical, you may want to wear a hairstyle or shirt that suggests the time period. If the character, for example, is a little outrageous, wear a bright color, but not a wild outfit. If the character is dominating or evil, wear black or gray. Never wear anything too overpowering, such as too much jewelry or a flashy tie or scarf. You are trying to sell yourself, and you do not want anything to distract from that. Keep makeup to a minimum. The directors will want to see the real you.

Be Energized

Go to bed early the night before an audition so that you can wake up feeling alert. Have a good breakfast, remembering to include protein. You do not know when you will be called to audition, and you want to have energy. You have no idea how long the auditioning session will last, so packing a snack is a good idea. Bring water. If you had a restless night's sleep, make every effort to be early for the audition, regardless of how much stress you may develop by rushing out the door. Still, be sure to have something to eat.

Getting There

Double-check the time and place. Arrive at least fifteen and as many as thirty minutes before the scheduled time. Make allowances for any possible travel delay. Being early shows the casting directors that you are reliable and committed. It also helps you relieve the stress of worrying about getting there in time. Arriving early also has the benefit of helping you find a spot to practice quietly.

Do not let other people in the lobby intimidate you. They are there with the same goals as you. Try to be pleasant and to not disturb others. You have to face it; you will be nervous. Being nervous is really an indication of how much you care about being there. If you try to disguise your butterflies with overconfidence, you may be off-putting or unconvincing and lose the part.

Singers/dancers perform together in an audition, each hoping to make the final cut.

The Audition

Bear in mind that you will likely have just five minutes to show what you can do. That means you must be ready to perform as soon as you are called. Music director and music supervisor Paul Christ has some auditioning tips in a story titled "20 Tips for Singing Auditions" published at musical-creations.com. Here is a summary of some things he suggests you do: Warm up wisely, and begin every day with humming and light vocal exercises you learned from your coach or singing teacher. Take a warm shower and do not talk. He says this will reduce swelling of the vocal cords. Breathe in through the nose and out through the mouth. Keep warm on the way to the audition and wear a hat and scarf "even in mildly cool weather. This helps keep your vocal muscles warm." Drink plenty of water. Bring a warm drink with you because the heat will help the areas around the larynx. Stay away from caffeine, which can dry you out.

Enter the venue and greet the directors and the accompanist. Pass the accompanist the sheet music. Let him or her know what tempo and key you would like the music to be played in. If there is no accompanist, bring a recording to back up your song. Be sure it is a high-quality recording, not too loud or overly instrumental. You should bring a recording anyway, just in case there is a problem with the accompanist. Some audition directors may want you to sing your song **a cappella**, meaning without musical accompaniment, so be prepared.

When your name is called, it is time to ignore distractions and focus on your music. Be as much in the character as you can, and sing!

Sometimes audition directors may want you to read from the script, thinking you might also be a good fit for an acting/singing role. He or she will give you a little background to the character or the scene to help you. You may be given a side, which is a short selection from the script. Sometimes you may get this when you arrive. Give it a good look. When auditioning, hold the side in front of you for quick reference. If you get lost and can't find your place in the script, stay calm and don't panic; no one wants an actor who melts down if something goes wrong.

Make sure your body is warm, stretched, and limber because the choreographer may want to see how well you can dance. He or she will perform some dance steps for you to follow. Do not worry—the dance steps are generally quite simple. More than anything, the casting director and choreographer want to see how well you can follow directions and how gracefully you can move across the stage. Unless the musical is focused on dance, such as *A Chorus Line* or *Chicago*, the dance audition will not be complicated. Another important tip is to make eye contact, smile, and use facial expressions while dancing. Even if you misstep, keep the smile and your positive attitude.

Your First Steps

Nearly everyone begins his or her theater singing career in the chorus. Sometimes the chorus is small, and that is called an ensemble. Ensemble singers will also play bit parts in a play. You may audition for a bigger role, and the director instead decides you are a perfect fit for the chorus.

Choruses in bigger-budget productions are larger, and people are cast only to sing and/or dance and have no speaking parts. A chorus audition happens in one day. Everyone is scheduled at the same time. First you perform your audition song for the music director. Once you have made that cut or cuts, you line up with other hopefuls for the dance part of the audition. In this, everyone participates at the same time. You are literally shoulder-to-shoulder with your competition. The choreographer will show you a small routine and watch how well you follow directions and how well you engage the invisible audience and interact with the other performers.

Then, the tension gets into full swing. People rejected for a chorus line do not get the bad news at home by phone. Rejection happens instantaneously.

First, the casting directors call for people to come forward, indicating people with a particular body type, or pointing and saying, "You, you, you, you, you, and you," and so forth, "step forward." At that point, everyone else goes home. If you are among those chosen, you will sing and dance again. Then the directors will call out for other attributes, such as hair color or ethnicity. Again, you sing and dance, and the directors continue choosing and eliminating. Says Jewels Nation, a longtime theater singer, "A chorus audition is a brutal, grueling, all-day marathon." But if you make it to the final "step forward," she says, "you are delirious."

Some singers stay with chorus-line work their entire career. In the theater, they are known as

A chorus rehearses a song before going off book and working onstage.

"gypsies," as they are in and out of numerous productions. Every chorus has a dance captain who manages the group and knows all the choreography.

Good Manners

Don't practice out loud backstage. It disturbs others. Avoid chatting backstage. Be friendly and supportive of other actors and singers. You do not want to start off on the wrong foot with a future cast member. Do not use your cell phone or slouch backstage. Clap when other performers have completed their audition.

Always be polite. Greet the casting directors and the accompanist. Listen well. If you do not understand a direction, you may ask a question. Afterward, thank the director(s) for the opportunity to audition and the accompanist for his or her assistance. Do not linger backstage long after your audition. You may remain for a little while, in case the directors call you back for another tryout. Never ask "How did I do?"

After the Audition

If you thought you couldn't be any more nervous than before your audition, think again. Often, it is after the audition that is the most unnerving time. Of course, you will be hoping to hear back from the directors with good news right away. But if you have a chance, what you will get is a callback. This means the directors liked something about you and want to see more. It could be they liked your singing but want to see if you can handle a speaking or dancing part as well. It could be that they are having a difficult time choosing between you and other singers.

A callback might come just after your audition, the next day, a couple of days later, or after a week or more. Be patient, but if you do not hear, do not torment yourself. Just move on.

If you do get a callback, keep in mind that they are calling you back because they liked something about you. So, do not vary much from your original audition. Wear similar clothing and style your hair the same way. While you should practice a few new songs from your cover book, it is much more likely you will be asked to perform songs from the show itself. Be sure to print out any new sheet music for your accompanist.

Research

Research is essential to any audition. Know your character. Focus on the character and his or her needs and feelings while you sing and perform. Without research, you will not be able to express your character with any depth, and even worse, you will not impress the audition director in the least.

Know the big picture. It is important to be familiar with the whole play. Make sure you know the play's plot, themes, and time period. If there is a cast recording, listen to it. More than likely a streaming service such as Spotify, Apple Music, or YouTube will help if you cannot track down a CD. If you can find a film of a live production, watch it. If it is a popular play, such as *Into the Woods* or *Little Shop of Horrors*, it may have been adapted as a movie. Some people believe seeing a movie version is counterproductive. Often times this is because movie directors may make significant changes to the show. As an example, in the movie version of *West Side Story* the order of some songs was changed, dialogue was rewritten, and a character named Ice was added. In other cases, songs will be cut altogether, or new songs will be added. Deciding to watch a movie version is up to you.

Sometimes in an audition, the director may consider casting you in a different role from the role you came to audition for. In this case, he or she may ask you to perform another song. Be as flexible as possible.

A singer practices her songs while listening to a cast recording.

Decision

It goes without saying that you will hear "no" a lot more than "yes" when trying for singing roles. Auditioning is challenging, but you must keep a positive outlook on both the experience and yourself, your talent, and your goals. Remember that if you did your best, you can be proud. And if you believe you made a mistake, accept and learn from it. There are many reasons for not being chosen that may have nothing to do with who you are or how you performed. Rejection is part of any performer's life, and there is no reason to expect otherwise. What you should expect is to have faith in yourself that your next audition will be even better and that parts will come.

College Applications or Remote Auditions

Sometimes you will be auditioning some distance away from the musical's venue. If you are applying to college or an internship program, it can also be far away. While it may be in your best interest to appear in person, it is generally acceptable in these circumstances to audition with a video. Be sure that the video quality is high and that the person filming you is well qualified. More videos these days are submitted as a download from a streaming service or website. Make the link clear and easy to find. Some institutions will also accept a hard copy application, résumé, and DVD or flash drive. Keep in mind that if you receive interest and a callback, you should make every effort to appear in person.

Getting Started

You have aced your audition and are holding in your hands a copy of the sheet music and the script. Your work now takes a new turn. After you meet with the directors and the creative team, you will need to absorb your character and enmesh yourself in the entire play. The more that you understand about your character, the more powerful you will be onstage. By singing, you will add greater depth to your character and have more impact on the play as a whole. An old adage, often applied to musical theater, is that actors break out into song when speaking their lines just isn't enough. Make your character resonate by getting to know him or her (or IT, such as Audrey II, the plant in *Little Shop of Horrors*). Some questions to ask yourself might be:

- Where has this character been?
- What is he or she doing now?
- Where is he or she going?
- How old is the character?
- Does the character have a job?
- Is he or she married or single or divorced or widowed?
- Is there a problem that the character is working through?
- Is any decision coming out of the song?
- Is the character wishing for something?

- Has the character lost something?

- Who is the character talking to—who is the song for?

- What is the character's state of mind? Is the character happy, sad, angry, confused, determined, spirited, joyful, lonely?

Rehearsals

Directors begin rehearsals with a **table read.** Generally, the director and the cast will sit together in a room (not necessarily around a table) with the script and read the play. Often, the lyrics of the songs will also be read out loud. The goal is to make everyone familiar with the plot, theme, and context of the play, as well as the characters' relationships with each other. Even if you do not have a speaking role, everyone should be present. Even if you don't have lines, you will still have to be in character when you are onstage. The table read gives people a chance to ask questions about the play and gives the director the opportunity to describe his or her vision. The director will also give background on the play, such as explaining that the musical *West Side Story* is a modern retelling of Shakespeare's *Romeo and Juliet*, set in a changing neighborhood in New York City. After several table reads, actors get a better feel for their lines, and everyone has a good grasp on the flow of the play. During these rehearsals, the director will distribute a schedule and assign the date that the cast must be **off book**—that is, when everyone must have memorized their lines.

Everyone is expected to bring their copy of the script and a pencil (not pen) to all rehearsals. Changes happen every day. You are responsible for taking note of changes, and not just those that involve you. Directors will give you personal tips, suggestions, and **blocking** directions, which you should also record. Many singers bring a recording device to practice. You should keep your script and your sheet music organized in a binder.

The music director holds rehearsals similar to table reads. He or she provides background to the play and expresses his or her vision on how the music and/or dance will pull the play together. Singers first read their song lyrics aloud and then begin singing along with the music director. Do not worry if you cannot sight-read your songs. Many singers do not. Instead, they use their recording devices. In the earliest practices, when singers are first learning and practicing their songs, recordings are used as accompaniment because there is a great deal of stopping and repeating. The music director will teach the music, tempo, tone, and harmonies. If you are having trouble with a particular interval, find a piano, play the musical phrase slowly, and sing along until the notes come naturally. Like the director, the music director will also assign an off-book date.

Before each rehearsal and before you practice at home, you need to warm up your voice. Just as you would stretch before running a marathon, you need to loosen your vocal cords and body. This is essential to protect your voice and help you produce your best-quality sound. Doctors, singing instructors, and other specialists offer a variety of useful warm-up exercises.

Singers use sheet music only in early rehearsals.

They vary from humming, trilling your tongue, and blowing through your lips to make a sound like a revving engine. Other warm-ups include face muscle and tongue exercises, scales, and singing the same note from a whisper to a boom.

When you begin practicing on your own outside of rehearsal, it is a good idea to listen to the rehearsal recordings while you do so. This helps keep you in line with the music director's expectations. Learning your songs takes effort. Begin by reading the lyrics out loud. Most people work at memorizing one song at a time. Recite the lyrics while listening to the music. After you have mastered the lyrics, cement them in your memory by singing the songs as fast as you can while doing something else, such as cleaning the house, taking a shower, or riding in the car.

A LEGENDARY TRIPLE THREAT

Dolores Conchita Figueroa del Rivero was born in Washington, DC. When she was seven, her father, a saxophonist from Puerto Rico who played in the US Navy Band, passed away. She turned to singing and dancing to fill the void. At age fifteen, a teacher encouraged her to audition for the New York City Ballet school. She was accepted and was awarded

Chita Rivera has had a long and rewarding career, beginning with the role of Anita in *West Side Story*.

a scholarship. Dolores also took voice lessons and discovered that she could sing as well as she could dance. At eighteen, she accompanied a friend on her way to an audition. Dolores decided to try out, too, and she was cast in the chorus. After touring with the company, she decided a career in musical theater was for her and adopted the stage name Chita Rivera.

Chita Rivera's breakout role was as the feisty Anita in *West Side Story*. When Chita Rivera sang Anita's song "I Like to Be in America," she became the talk of the town. *West Side Story* ran for 732 performances and produced an award-winning cast album. More Broadway hits followed for her, such as *Bye, Bye Birdie, Chicago, Sweet Charity, Flower Drum Song,* and *Kiss of the Spider Woman,* for which she won a **Tony Award**. In 2002, she became the first Hispanic woman to be awarded a Kennedy Center Honor. In 2009, she was awarded the Presidential Medal of Freedom from Barack Obama for lifetime artistic achievement. In 2015, at age eighty-two, she was nominated for a Tony for Best Leading Actress in a Musical for *The Visit*.

The director will post the rehearsal schedule backstage, along with the **callboard**, which is a daily listing of changes and developments. The rehearsal schedule may vary. You will see that unless you have a principal role, you will not be required at every rehearsal. Some rehearsals are for cast members with speaking roles only; others are for principals only. Some are only for singers and musicians and/or dancers. Others are only for dancers. Sometimes, groups will rehearse in different areas. Not until later in the process will there be all-cast rehearsals. Rehearsals for speaking and singing will include blocking, staging, and music, before the performers are off book. Technical rehearsals and dress rehearsals follow. Whatever the schedule calls for, be early. The time posted for rehearsals is start time, not arrival time. Theater lore says, "Ten minutes early is on time. On time is late."

You will have most of your rehearsals with the music director. If you are in a small production, such as those at most high schools, then you will have rehearsals with the director but at different times than the rest of the speaking-only cast. Once you and the other singers are comfortable with the lyrics, an accompanist (usually a piano player) will attend rehearsals with you. In most musicals, singers also have some dancing parts. In that case, you will attend choreography rehearsals as well. After several separate rehearsals, singers and dancers will practice together. By this time, the director of the orchestra will join rehearsals to pick up things to pass on to the musicians. When dress rehearsals are approaching, singers and dancers will practice with the orchestra.

Final Rehearsals

After cast members are comfortable with their lines, songs, and dances, blocking and staging are added. Blocking is the positioning of cast members onstage. It includes when and from where a character comes onto the stage, and when and where the character stands, sits, kneels, or moves across the stage. Choreography is also blocked within an area of the stage. Staging includes positioning but also cast members' movements, such as kicking or waving. It also includes characters' interactions and how their props are handled. Staging also encompasses set constructions, lighting, and sound. Typical rehearsal schedule language includes notices such as, "Speaking roles called for blocking," "All called for blocking and music," "Dancers called for choreography," and "Singers called for blocking and staging."

As opening night approaches, other production departments become a part of rehearsals. There are technical-only rehearsals for the lighting and sound departments. Next there are "wet tech" rehearsals that include lighting, sound, and the cast. In these rehearsals, singers interact closely with the technical departments. The sound people are responsible for making sure singers can be heard without distortion throughout the theater. Lighting technicians work with singers in order to help emphasize the impact lighting has on your singing performance. Light technicians follow your movements while the director positions you as you sing, speak, and dance.

Closer to opening night, all-cast, all-music, and all-crew rehearsals will go through one act at a time

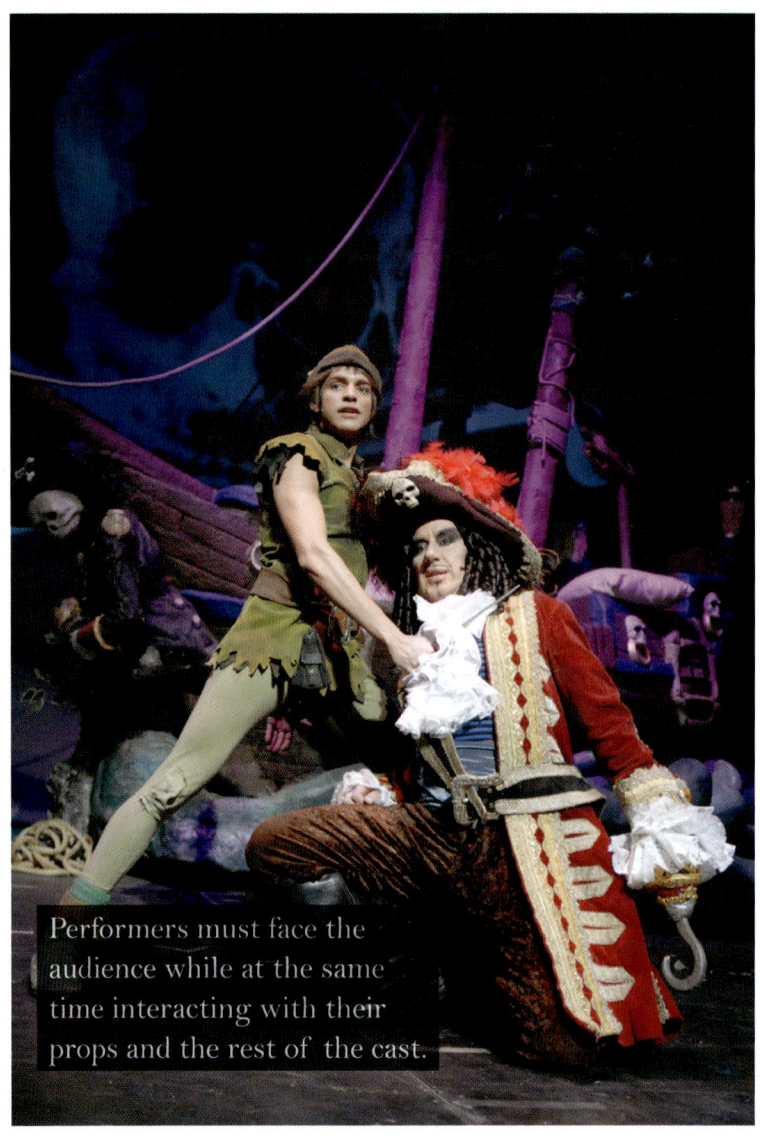

Performers must face the audience while at the same time interacting with their props and the rest of the cast.

together. Full rehearsals include the entire cast, the technical departments, and the orchestra or stage musicians. Dress rehearsals are the final rehearsals. In these, the cast rehearses the entire play in full costume from start to finish, with the musicians, technicians, and stagehands.

When the performance is ready to begin, the director and the music director often leave. Their work is done, and now the production is up to you and the rest of the cast and crew. The stage manager remains in charge. It is his or her job to be sure everyone in the production is present, and that all props and set materials are in order. The stage manager will maintain the prompt book, oversee cleanliness and safety precautions, and be responsible for any emergencies. It is the stage manager whom you go to if there is an issue or serious concern.

The Curtain Rises

As a singer, your role in a musical gives the production its spark and passion. You are not only speaking words, you are doing so with intensity. Remember, in theater, actors sing when simply speaking is not enough. But before you sing, you must let your speaking voice rise on a crescendo, so that when you break into song, it is not a sharp departure from the play. This is not easy, but you have practiced for this moment.

As you sing, you need to engage any cast members onstage with you, while also pulling the audience into your musical message. To do this, you must always face the audience while at the same time looking at the character or characters you are singing to or singing and dancing with. You will also face the audience as naturally as possible while you interact with any props.

Sing with a sense of freedom onstage. Be ready for anything. Each night will feel like a different performance. The cast members will deliver their lines and perform their songs and dances with a different feel during each performance. The audience is a different creature, too. A receptive audience will ramp up everyone's performance. On the other hand, an audience that is a little bit harder to reach may make the performer in all of you rise to the occasion and win them over.

Taking Your Bow

When the show closes each night, before you completely collapse, you must accept your reward—applause. But curtain calls should be smooth and quick. The curtain closes when the play ends, and the cast exits the stage before returning to take a bow. Even bows must be rehearsed; no one wants to bump into each other or enter out of order. The director decides which cast members should come out when. If it is a large cast, groups of people such as the chorus will come out together, take their bows, and wait for the next group, until the principals and leads take their own bows. Small casts generally take their bows individually. To reach out to the audience, performers look directly at the audience and often take themselves out of character. Many do so by removing a part of their costume—such as a hat or jacket—or letting down their hair. Once all the cast members are onstage, they redirect the applause by gesturing toward the musicians and sometimes the lighting and sound crews.

The curtain call and the audience applause is every performer's greatest reward.

The Final Curtain

The run is done. The curtain falls for the last time. After a few rounds of backstage hugs and congratulations, it is time to **strike**. Strike, the opposite of **load-in**, is a term describing what comes after every final performance. Load-in is the term for the day about a week before the production opens when everyone gives a hand carrying in the equipment, sets, props, and costumes. Strike is load-in in reverse, and there are no disappearing acts. Right after the show, unless it is a major, big-budget show, everyone participates in taking down and packing up. After strike is over, if people have the energy, the cast and crew come together for a party.

Debuting on a London stage, a principal singer and the chorus perform in *High School Musical*.

CHAPTER FOUR

High Hopes

So you have performed in your high school play and discovered a passion for singing in theater. Should you follow your passion? The answer is yes because today a career in musical theater is not an impossible dream. Millions of people are hoping to find careers in the performing arts, especially musical careers. The popularity of a singing career has been spreading in part because of music streaming and television shows such as *American Idol*, *High School Musical*, *Glee*, and *The Voice*. More inspirational to you, however, is the increasing popularity and recognition of new, modern, and innovative Broadway musicals, such as *Hamilton*, *Dear Evan Hansen*, and *Wicked*. This increase in popularity has opened up many more opportunities for a singing career onstage.

Tough Road

Even with the new excitement surrounding musical theater, developing a career as a singer in musical theater is a big challenge. It takes an undue amount of determination, talent, grit, and self-discipline to succeed. Rhoda Jacobs, a former singer and theater performer, emphatically adds luck to that equation. Luck, of course, is more elusive, almost completely out of your control. Secretly, every singer fantasizes about getting "discovered" by chance, whether by singing karaoke in a club, via a YouTube clip, or meeting a producer at a party. But of course, those encounters rarely come to pass. According to Jacobs, "Instant fame is not a reality." Of course, people try to get close to luck by seeking out others in the business who have good connections in the theater world. They keep their "spark" alive, their hopes up, and nurture a willingness to take risks.

Higher Education

Twenty-five or so years ago, a degree in the theater arts was extremely rare. Most who wanted one studied at theater or acting schools or at music conservatories in large cities. Today, many colleges and universities around the country offer theater degrees, even specifically ones in musical theater. With so many people on and around campus sharing the same interests in music and theater, you will make many valuable connections. Some people will expand your musical and cultural horizons and others may open up doors for future theater employment.

Many people will have financial concerns about pursuing a musical theater degree in college. There are scholarships and financial aid available for theater programs, but you will need to use your talent and audition skills to wow the admissions department. The idea of going to college to study is a double-edged sword. It is expensive without a scholarship.

It will be difficult to pay off student loans with the starting wages of a singer and theater performer. Furthermore, people your age who are not in college are out there gaining experience on you.

On the other hand, a school with a good drama/music/theater department offers many benefits. First, you will meet many people who share your interests. Campuses are a fountain of information and inspiration. The more people you get to know, the more resources you will have at hand. Networking with other singers, dancers, and actors will help advance your career in a variety of ways.

Besides thorough training, theater programs offer experience through a variety of student productions. Competition for these productions is just as rigorous as in the professional and semiprofessional theater world. Only the best will be onstage. Scouts and agents may attend these performances, especially the

Schools such as Emerson College stage showcases so graduating seniors can perform for agents.

ORDEAL BY FIRE

"Don't put me through this ordeal by fire!" sings the leading lady in *The Phantom of the Opera*. The operetta is one of the most passionate ever produced. To summarize the plot: A new theater company takes over an old theater. Living in the darkness below the theater is a disfigured and embittered Phantom. He falls in love with the company's leading lady. She, however, has a lover of whom the Phantom is murderously jealous. In a final scene, the Phantom ties a noose around the lover's neck.

The Phantom is a demanding, and sometimes dangerous, role.

Thomas James O'Leary starred as the Phantom on Broadway for 774 performances. In a performance with a touring company before moving to Broadway, his adaptability as a true performer came vividly to light.

In the final scene of the operetta, the Phantom, despite all his fury, decides to cut the lover's noose by burning through the rope with a candle. O'Leary's prop was a trick candle. But one night as he took hold of the candle, a spark landed on his bald "wig." The wig had been oiled so that his "bald" head shined. The spark and the oil set O'Leary's head on fire. Yet, he continued to rage, all the while pounding his head and singing, "Go now! … Just take her and go … Go now, and leave me!" Stagehands were ready with fire extinguishers, but he put the fire out with his hands. He was told that he had a crown of flames 4 inches (10 centimeters) high. O'Leary said later he overheard a woman from the audience say, "My favorite part was when his head caught on fire!"

senior class productions. Sometimes schools have showcases just for scouts and agents. Shine, and you will be seen. Another major benefit of a higher education is providing you with the ability to be hired for a well-paying supplemental job in education or in business. You may have to have a second career or job before your musical career gets into full swing. Additionally, when you decide to end or pull back on theater performing, you will have an education that will help you enter other fields of work.

Single, Double ... Now Triple Threat

Up until the 1980s, the notion of being a triple threat was almost nonexistent. Many performers specialized in just one talent. They were either singers, dancers, or actors. True, some of the better performers in musical theater were known for their ability to act and sing, or sing and dance, but being able to sing, act, and dance well was a rarity. Those with the talent of Gene Kelly (*Singin' in the Rain*) became movie stars. Today, in large part, it is a necessity. Singers are especially affected by this. Musical theater is on the rise, and so is the competition.

Most singers start out early knowing they love singing. As young children, you will hear them singing along to songs on the radio, TV, movies, videos, and online streams. Although they may be born with natural talent, that is only the beginning. Training makes the natural talent develop, and as it does, the excitement of achievement lures many to choose a career in musical theater. Singing well is only the first hurdle. Learning to act and dance with skill will require a great deal more training and practice. If you discover early a passion for singing, it is best to begin training in acting and dance right away because you will need all three skills.

Audition Trials

Auditions are a test, but many feel they are more closely like a trial. And often they are. Casting directors get overwhelmed and exhausted by the repetition. A steady stream of eager faces and voices can begin to blur together after a long day. Often, the casting directors are cool and abrupt, making it hard on you while your hopes are high and your ego may be wavering. From the perspective of the judge/casting director, he or she does not want to waste his or her time, nor yours. From your perspective, the best defense you can mount is an amazing five minutes of your finest work.

Beyond your performance, you must also be prepared for the unknown. You have brought in your song and your cover book. You have sung your heart out. But the casting director wants to test your acting skills. You are handed a script, but it is not one from the character or play that you were expecting. The director wants you to do a **cold read**, to test your adaptability. A cold read is one where you have never laid eyes on what you are asked to enact. Not easy. Breathe deep and focus. Read loudly, clearly, and with poise. More than anything, they are looking for self-confidence. Next could be the dance audition. Hopefully, you will have dressed appropriately. Don't wear stiff jeans or anything bulky. Wear tights, dance skirts, or shorts, as well as jazz shoes or some other smooth-soled shoe. Be prepared!

Rejection

Too much cannot be said about the need to be very thick-skinned if you want a career in the arts. Rejection hurts, and it generally comes often. You may spend more time auditioning than working. But auditioning is work, too. When the callback does not come, "What did I do wrong?" will probably be your first reaction. If you think you were rejected for good cause, learn from that mistake and improve your auditioning style. But just as likely, you did nothing wrong. Directors may have decided that they wanted someone older, younger, taller, or shorter, or for some other reason they did not see you as right for the role.

When the rejection comes, you will feel awful. It is a natural response, and best not to ignore it. Go ahead and feel bad. Punch your pillow. Cry. Listen to loud music; yell and stomp. But you cannot dwell or survive on negative feelings. Move on. Call a friend, go for a walk, take a bike ride, do a crossword puzzle, go to the gym, eat ice cream. Do anything that helps you get back on track for your next audition. If it happens while you are still in high school, don't get discouraged. Remember, you are not alone; it happens to everyone. "Everyone has dry spells," says Jewels Nation. "You have to ride it out."

It is important to care for your voice every way you can by resting your vocal cords and keeping your throat warm and moist.

Guarding Your Instrument

Besides staying physically fit, you need to take care of your voice, your prized musical instrument. Many younger singers belt out their favorite tunes long before they have been trained to do so safely. Never sing without first warming up. If you have been performing nightly and your voice becomes hoarse or your throat hurts, you are singing incorrectly and have strained your voice. Singing is not painful for a well-trained voice. You will need to rest. Talk to your vocal coach or your choir director and ask him or her to assess your voice and prepare special warm-ups. Sleep as much as you can, and ignore the temptation to go out after the show or rehearsal. Spend as much of your downtime as possible not speaking. Consult a doctor if your voice worsens. Ben Platt, the Tony-winning star of *Dear Evan Hansen*, sings his role with phenomenal intensity. To be in top form for his next performance, he sleeps ten hours a night and takes advantage of any break from performing. During a recent break, he said he went to his apartment and enjoyed "twenty hours of mouth-shutting."

Stage Fright

Not only do beginners get nervous before the curtain rises, but experienced performers can also be struck with the jitters. Singers believe that if you can get through your first line, everything will come easily afterward. Keeping your throat moist and stretching your body can help loosen your muscles and steady your nerves. Some singers suggest making up a question that can be answered by your first line. For example, the first line of the first song in *Thoroughly Modern Millie* is, "I studied all the pictures in the magazines and books." If those were your lines, before you came onstage you could ask yourself, "What did I do in the bookstore?" Most helpful of all to combat stage fright is to remember all the times people praised you for your talent.

Oh, Woe

Most singers who choose a career in theater say they could not think of doing anything else. But the hard facts are that the career is a challenging and emotional roller coaster. It is a career requiring the

Summer stock theater is often performed outdoors, and it is a great avenue for gaining experience.

utmost patience, perseverance, and physical stamina. Regardless of how down or exhausted you feel, the show, as they say, must go on. It is physically draining to act, sing, and dance with passion and intensity for hours, night after night. Performance also takes its toll on family and social life. Many performers are away from home a lot. Not only do rehearsals fill the better part of the weeks and months leading up to the performance, but many theater people work away from home. Some performers work in a touring company, others do **summer stock** far from home, while still others perform nightly on cruise ships all around the world.

WATCH WHAT YOU SAY

Theater has some strange rules to follow. Many of them are built around superstitions. Be mindful of these:

- Never say "Macbeth" in a theater.

- Never peek around the curtain to look at the audience.

- Say "break a leg," not "good luck," when wishing someone success.

- No whistling.

The prospects for earning a decent income in musical theater are not at all guaranteed. Some singers are out of work for long periods of time. Wages are low. However, wages do increase once you earn more credits and can be accepted into the actors' union, called Actors' Equity. Then, you will be paid on a union scale, and it is guaranteed that you will be paid even if the show closes early. However, you can only work in all-union productions, where the competition is very stiff.

You should be prepared, especially in the early stages of your career, to work another job. But it may be hard to find a job that gives you flexibility to be available to audition and, hopefully, rehearse and perform once you have gotten a part. If you decide to satisfy your stage urge in community theater, then you will have to find a job that lets you work and perform.

Competition in a singing career in theater is becoming more intense. There are so many more schools, colleges, and universities offering theater and music studies than ever before. The number of talented graduates increases every year. Fortunately, there is more work than ever before. But you must stay on your toes, be vigilant and resourceful, and keep current.

Breaking Up

Nearly everyone suffers when a production ends. After weeks and months of spending long and intense hours together every day, the cast and crew have bonded. They have supported one another, laughed and clashed with one another, and have sung and danced with each other, and together they have produced a living, breathing artistic creation. Cast, musicians, and crew work so closely they feel like family. But when the final curtain falls, the cord is cut and the theater family comes apart. Most performers say that it takes weeks to get over the sadness and feeling of loss.

Small theaters, whether community or regional, offer opportunities to perform. Many productions are new works.

CHAPTER FIVE
What Comes Next

Broadway may be every singer's dream, but chances are most singers will not attain the heights of Broadway in New York or the West End in London. Yet many exciting and fulfilling opportunities await outside of these illustrious venues.

Many aspiring singers choose to move to a big city noted for theater—New York, Chicago, Toronto, London, or Los Angeles. (Los Angeles is more of a film town than a theater town, but there are still many opportunities there to sing in live theater.) Competition may be stiff in the big cities, but there are hundreds of venues and productions, and a great deal of support and enthusiasm for the performing arts. Many famous musicals began in small **off-Broadway** theaters. For example, *Hamilton* began at the Public Theater in 2015, came to Broadway in 2016, and won eleven Tony Awards, including Best Musical. Tony Awards are awards given to live theater performers and productions on Broadway, the theater equivalent of the Academy Awards.

Small professional or semiprofessional theaters are found throughout the country. You will likely be starting out in community theater. It may surprise you how professional and rewarding community theater can be. Auditions are serious business, and you may have two or three callbacks before you are cast. Rehearsals will be held on nights and weekends, and attendance is mandatory. It will be up to you to juggle work, family, and rehearsals. Other opportunities are with touring companies that travel around the country and perform at regional theaters. Summer stock, which is theater performed only during the summer and usually in outdoor locations, is also a wonderful opportunity, especially for students who may have summers off. Other venues to consider are theme park theaters, dinner theaters, and cruise ships.

Other Choices

Cruise ship theater may come as a surprise. Once the venue for lightweight, amateur-seeming productions, cruise ships now put on multimillion-dollar productions of popular musicals and attract and hire talented performers. The shows are all union productions, meaning that the pay and benefits are reliable and financially rewarding. If you love musical theater and want the opportunity to travel, you might look no further than cruise line audition notices. Some cruise lines specifically feature musical theater as their big draw to customers. You will earn respect and have a thoroughly professional experience.

Dinner theater is another way to pursue your career. At dinner theaters, which are numerous throughout the country, theatergoers enjoy fine dining and afterward watch a play. Amy Adams, a film star known for leading roles in *Enchanted*, *Arrival*, and *Her*, began her career in dinner theater in Colorado and Minnesota. She said the other performers were "stunning and awesome" singers and dancers. She also said that after years working in film, she "pined" for singing in dinner theater, where she worked with people she thought of as family. She appreciated that the work was regular and well paying. Adams returned to live theater in New York with the role of the Baker's Wife in *Into the Woods*.

Difficult Roles

Not every musical theater career is in front of the lights. Most everyone knows what an understudy is: a person who learns the role of a performer and fills in when the performer is unable to appear onstage. Understudies rehearse the roles of their assigned person and spend nearly all their time backstage, as relative unknowns. But some careers have been born when an understudy is called to take over. Taye Diggs is a talented singer and dancer who started his career at Busch Gardens in Williamsburg, Virginia. He was an understudy in a revival of *Carousel* when a principal fell ill. His performance soon earned him the lead in *Rent*. Sutton Foster was an understudy in *Thoroughly Modern Millie* in Los Angeles. When

Taye Diggs got his break as an understudy when the lead actor fell ill.

the lead fell ill, she took over the role and won a Tony Award.

While many people are familiar with the role of an understudy, most people outside the theater world have never heard of a **swing**. But musical theater people consider them the "superstars" of any production. A swing learns every musical role—every song sung by every singer and every dance danced by every dancer. The singers and dancers onstage sing in finely tuned harmony and dance in finely choreographed formations. They also usually have several costume changes. A swing must step in, often at a moment's notice, and imitate exactly the work of the performer she or he is replacing.

Side Jobs

It is often said in musical theater, and in the arts and performing arts in general, that either you make a living at it or you do not. If you do make a living, you again have two paths—a good living or a financially rocky one. Yet either way, it is likely that because you are living your dream, you are satisfied. But to stay in the game, many people need to find a "day job" to supplement their income. Those with college backgrounds often teach. Others, who need flexibility not found in a nine-to-five job, wait tables, work for arts groups, or do fundraising or freelance marketing. Some find employment in advertising, working as film extras, or doing background singing and dancing for music videos. Lucrative careers in advertising for singers include singing jingles for commercials and

Many music majors enjoy a career in music education and perform in the summer.

voice-over work. Jewels Nation, who sang and danced on Broadway as a teenager, found that she needed to supplement her theater career with voice-over work. "Everyone wanted me, I could do a great 'Valley Girl,'" she says.

What You Are

Musical theater is more than singing show tunes and tap dancing across the stage. It is hard, demanding work that requires perseverance, physical fitness, stamina, talent, and creativity. You can sing. You can memorize lines, lyrics, rhythms, and tempos. You can dance—modern, jazz, tap, and ballet. You are a compelling actor. You inspire, entertain, and inform your audience. You bring characters, ideas, and stories to life. You bring pleasure, laughter, meaning, and emotion to people's lives. You can do it night after night, unfailingly. You have the ability and desire to consistently learn something new. You have charm, dedication, and passion. Singers and theater performers want to please their audiences and will do everything in their power to make it happen.

What You Can Do

As you go through the process of becoming an experienced singer and performer, have you ever stopped to think about what might be the hidden skills and qualities you are developing? If you step away from a career in performing, what else might you be qualified to do? Employers in all fields generally have two ways of looking at what they want from employees. They either want people who can perform a specialized skill, such as a surgeon or a plumber, or they are looking for employees who have desirable traits that can help a business be more creative and competitive.

First and foremost, you have oral communication skills. You have a trained, appealing voice. You can speak clearly, thoughtfully, and articulately. Being onstage has taught you to be comfortable speaking in public and with groups. You come from a fast-paced environment and have learned how to be clear, respectful, and precise in your communications with others backstage. Many employers not only rely on their employees with communication skills, but they often sponsor workshops to help their employees improve their communication skills.

Second, you are a highly creative person. You know how to use your creativity to solve problems. With each role you portrayed, you took a fresh look at an existing character and made it new. Business,

A DREAM OF BROADWAY

Since she was seven years old, Randi Zuckerberg wanted to star on Broadway. She sang her way through childhood and performed in front of friends

> Randi Zuckerberg, while being the head of a major media company, never forgot her love of singing in musical theater.

82 Singing in Theater

and family in school productions. She took piano and classical singing lessons and applied to Harvard's music department. She said her "dreams came crashing down" when she was not accepted into the music department. She continued to sing, using the stage name Randi Jayne. Zuckerberg graduated from Harvard with a degree in psychology and became one of the first few people hired by Facebook. She ran marketing for the company. Her skills as a performer helped the little company gain traction far better and faster than what her brother, Mark, Facebook's founder, could have accomplished.

Randi Zuckerberg went on to become the founder and CEO of a media company, Zuckerberg Media, and she is the creator of Dot Complicated, an online forum that considers the role of technology in modern life. But she never gave up her dream to perform in musical theater. Zuckerberg continued to sing and even started a band. In 2015, she auditioned and won a role in *Rock of Ages* on Broadway. She later had a small part in *Anything Goes* in San Francisco. She is a successful author, philanthropist, entrepreneur, and public speaker. She never gave up her love for music and the stage. She is a supporter of musical theater and is a Tony Award voter. In a TED Talk, she explained that success in one part of your life does not take away your dreams in another.

marketing, and technology companies look for that "outside the box" way of approaching problems and developing new products.

You have numerous qualities, almost too many to mention. Here are a few more:

You know how to complete a task on time, without taking shortcuts. Consider opening night. You are ready, your colleagues are ready; you have overcome every obstacle and taken care of every detail. You have gotten the job done and you have gotten it done on time.

You know how to work cooperatively with many different types of people. Just think of the variety of roles, jobs, and activities that go into a successful production. You and your colleagues know how to work together, to appreciate each other's abilities, and to be respectful, meanwhile working under enormous pressure. In any business, you could be the valuable team member who engages and encourages coworkers and helps them produce their best work.

Think of all the hours that you spent memorizing lyrics, learning dance steps, and practicing your lines. You know how to do an assigned task independently, a trait many employers need.

You would not have accomplished all that you have without your ability to schedule your time. In school, you had to balance classes, studies, rehearsals, and possibly a job. After school, you balanced rehearsals, a job, and preparations for auditions, not to mention voice lessons, physical fitness training, practice, and saving time to spend with friends and family. Time budgeting skills are extremely important to employers.

Think of the small-budget productions you have been a part of. There is not the luxury of months to put together a production. Some productions have but weeks to practice and organize. But you know how to memorize a script and learn the music and your dance routines quickly. You may dance around your living room, sing in the shower, and repeat your lines to yourself sitting on a bus, but you learn quickly.

Along with absorbing material quickly, you know how to be a good listener. You take direction, you keep notes, and you ask pertinent questions of the right people only when necessary.

You would not get past your first production if you did not know how to meet deadlines and be on time. As you know, these two requirements are set in stone in the theater profession. These are some of the most desirable traits employers look for.

It goes without saying you can work under pressure, without coming undone. You know how to persevere, bite your lip, and stay in control. You also know how to be flexible and roll with the punches. There are changes throughout rehearsals: songs change tempo, lines are rewritten, dances change, costumes and sets change. You jot these changes down in your binder and keep going forward.

You are polite to colleagues and respectful of authority. You know how to take the initiative to get something accomplished that needs accomplishing, but you get approval and you do not step on anyone's toes.

One of the biggest needs in the employment world today is marketing and sales whizzes. This is especially true in high-tech software marketing. Engineers produce innovative new products but have

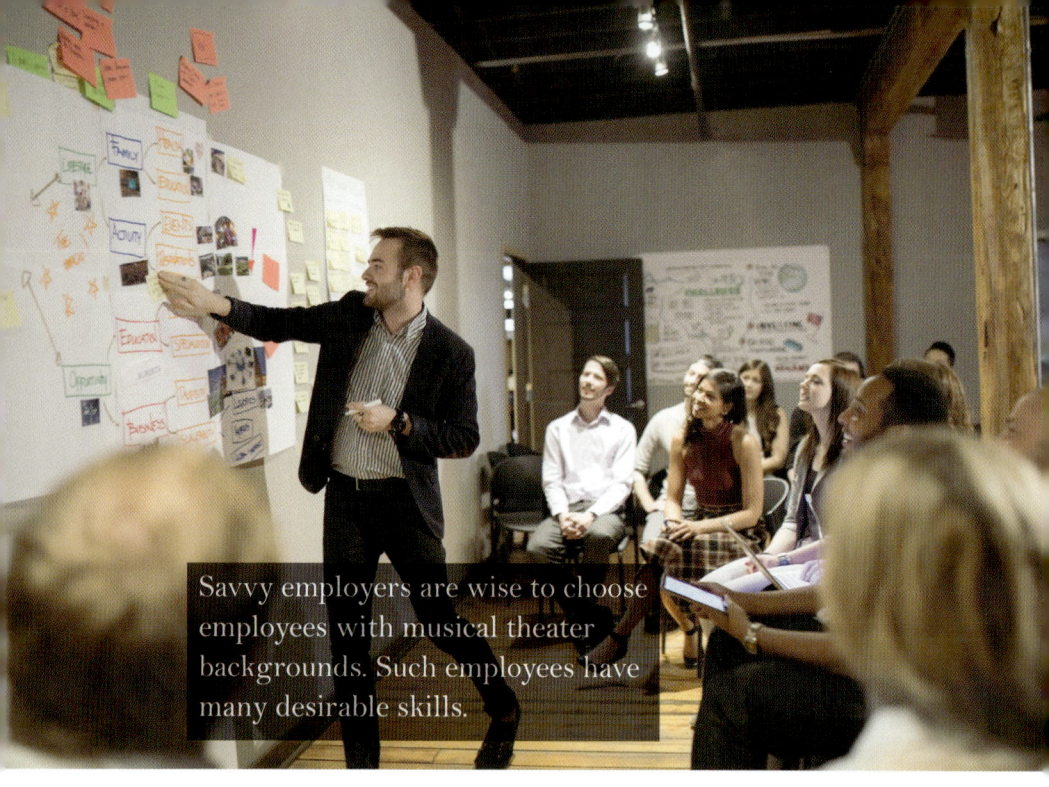

Savvy employers are wise to choose employees with musical theater backgrounds. Such employees have many desirable skills.

no idea how to make them appealing to consumers. That is where a talent like yours can make a small company turn successful and a large company grow even larger.

If you want to pursue a new career and stay focused on your voice, you may want to return to school and become accredited as a speech therapist, or you could provide music therapy for children. Or you could become a vocal coach or a music director. You could be a music director at a theater camp, run acting workshops, be a talent scout, or be a college recruiter or an admissions officer for the school's music and drama department.

The list of skills continues: goal-oriented, focused, dedicated, and self-disciplined. So, take a look at yourself and what you have become. Notice how many desirable attributes you have acquired. You would not be in the theater business if you did not have a healthy sense of your own worth. Think about how to use your many desirable traits to your advantage. If your many auditions have taught you nothing else, they have taught you how to sell yourself. So, take stock of your skills and accomplishments, and move wherever else you might want to go.

A career in musical theater may offer you everything you have wanted. But you need to decide for yourself what success means. Some singers equate success with fame. Many performers set their own goals and define their own idea of success. For some, it is getting cast in a desired role, performing in a certain theater, or working with a special performer or director. A career in musical theater might have many, many challenges, but as the lead performer in *A Chorus Line* sings, it is "what I did for love."

GLOSSARY

a cappella Singing without musical accompaniment.

accompanist Someone who is playing a musical instrument while someone else is singing or playing the main part. In an audition, it is the person who plays while and actor sings.

alto The lowest vocal range for a female.

audition The interview for a role as a singer, actor, dancer, or musician, consisting of a demonstration.

baritone The second-lowest vocal range for a male.

bass The lowest vocal range for a male.

belt A style of singing at a louder volume.

blocking The planning and working out of the movements of actors onstage.

callboard A backstage bulletin board on which notices of concern to the actors are posted.

cast recording An audio recording of the musical selections as performed by the original Broadway or Hollywood cast.

choreographer The person who composes the sequence of steps for dances and then directs the dancers and chorus members.

cold read A reading of a script done by actors who have not previously reviewed the play.

eleven o'clock number The most rousing song sung by the lead performer near the end of the show.

headshot A professional portrait that accompanies a résumé or is used in a playbill or other publicity for a show.

load-in To bring costumes, props, lights, sound equipment, and set materials into the theater.

mezzo-soprano The middle vocal range for a female.

off book The point where performers have memorized their lines or songs.

off Broadway Smaller professional theaters in New York which are not in the theater district.

pitch How high or low a note is. A singer with perfect pitch can recreate a note without a reference tone.

prompt book The book kept by the stage manager that contains notes on stage directions, cues for actors and sound and lighting technicians, and lines.

soprano The highest vocal range for a female.

strike To dismantle the set at the end of a show's run.

summer stock Theatrical productions done by repertory companies in the summer months near resorts or in big cities.

swing A performer who knows all the songs and dances and fills in for an absent performer.

table read A session where the cast reads the script out loud together.

tenor The highest vocal range for a male.

Tony Award An award recognizing excellence in live Broadway theater.

triple threat Someone who can sing, dance, and act.

vocal range The span from the lowest note to the highest note that a voice can attain.

FOR MORE INFORMATION

Books

Hall, Karen. *So You Want to Sing Music Theater: A Guide for Professionals.* Lanham, MD: Rowman & Littlefield, 2014.

Melton, Joan. *Singing in Musical Theater: The Training of Singers and Actors.* New York: Allworth Press, 2007.

Moore, Tracey, and Allison Bergman. *Acting the Song: Performance Skills for the Musical Theater.* New York: Allworth Press, 2016.

Shapiro, Eddie. *Nothing Like a Dame: Conversations with the Great Women of Musical Theater.* New York: Oxford University Press, 2014.

Online Articles

15 Amazing Pre-College Summer Theater Programs
https://www.backstage.com/advice-for-actors/resources/15-amazing-pre-college-summer-theater-programs
Writing for Backstage, KC Wright profiles summer programs for young performers.

Guide to Performing: Singing
https://www.theguardian.com/music/2009/may/10/tips-stage-performance-singing
This article from the *Guardian* features advice for an effective vocal performance onstage.

20 Tips for Singing Auditions
https://www.musical-creations.com/tips/auditioning/20-tips-prepare-singing-audition
Experienced music director Paul Christ offers suggestions for a successful vocal audition.

Websites

Broadway Musical Home
http://www.broadwaymusicalhome.com
A website listing the one hundred most popular Broadway musicals, with plot summaries, songs, lyrics, and information about actors, composers, and dancers.

Broadway or Bust Sneak Performances
http://www.pbs.org/wgbh/broadway-or-bust/watch/sneak-performances

Watch live theater performances of selected songs from musicals old and new.

The Musical Theater Performer
http://www.shmoop.com/careers/musical-theater-performer
An informative website covering multiple topics in a clear, easy-going style. Topics include: tools of the trade, qualifications, fame, stress, a typical day.

Videos

Highlights from the Public Theater's "Into the Woods," Part 1
https://www.youtube.com/watch?v=mBl-zOvRFCM
This Playbill video provides highlights from Stephen Sondheim and James Lapine's award-winning musical *Into the Woods*.

Mamie Parris Sings "Memory" from Cats on Broadway
https://www.youtube.com/watch?v=wxuNkemKWgU
This evocative song was performed by Mamie Parris in a revival of the musical *Cats* on Broadway.

INDEX

Page numbers in **boldface** are illustrations. Entries in **boldface** are glossary terms.

a cappella, 41
accompanist, 10–11, 15, 18–19, **20**, 21, 25, 32, 41, 44–45, 54
Actors' Equity, 72
Adams, Amy, 77
alto, 33
audition, 6–7, 10–11, 13–15–18, **28**, 29–34, 38–47, **38**, **40**, 52–53, 62, 67–68, 72, 76, 83–84, 87

ballad, 35–36
baritone, 34
bass, 34
belt, 33–34, 37, 69
blocking, 50, 54–55
blues, 36
breathing, 6, 8, 15–16, 23, 40, 67

callback, 44–45, 68, 76
callboard, 54
casting calls, 29–30
cast recording, 10, 45
choir, 5–6, **17**
choreographer, 9, 18–20, 25, 30, 41–42
chorus, 7–8, 19–22, **20**, 25–27, 30, 33, 36, 42–44, 53, 58, **60**
cold read, 67–68
contemporary musicals, 37
costumes, 18, 21–23, 56, 58–59, 79, 85
cruise ships, 71, 76
curtain call, 58, **59**

dancing, **11**, 12–13, 15, 19–21, 23, 25, 29–30, **40**, 41–44, 50, 52–55, 57–58, 66–68, 71, 79–80, 84–85
Dear Evan Hansen, 36, 61, 70
Diggs, Taye, 77, **78**
dinner theater, 76–77
director, 9, 18–21, 23–25, **24**, 34–35, 49–50, 54–55, 57–58

eleven o'clock number, **35**, 36–37

fitness, 13–15, 80, 84
Foster, Sutton, 77, 79

Hamilton, 36, 61, 75
headshot, 29, 30, **31**
hip-hop, 36–37

94 Singing in Theater

improvisation, 14
Into the Woods, 10, 33, 45, 77

jazz, 8, 15, 32, 36

legit musicals, 37
lighting, 18, 21–22, 55, 58
load-in, 59

makeup, 22, 38
marketing, 79–80, 83–86
mezzo-soprano, 33
microphones, 22–23
music director, 18–19, 22, 25, 30, 40, 42, 50–51, 54, 57, 86

off book, 49–50, 54
off Broadway, 75
orchestra, 18–19, 21, 25, 54, 56, 58

Phantom of the Opera, 32, 64–65, **64**
pitch, 6, 8, 16
pop/rock musicals, 33, 37
posture, 6, 8, 14
prompt book, 20–21, 57

rehearsals, 10, **11**, 13, 15, **17**, 19, **20**, 21, 23–25, **24**, **43**, 49–51, **51**, 54–56, 58, 71, 76–77, 84–85
rejection, 42–43, 47, 68
Rent, **26**, 27, 34, 37, 77
research, 10, 12, 45–46
résumé, 10, 12, 29–31, 47

Rivera, Chita, 52–53, **52**
rock, 8, 15, 33, 36–37

sets, 18, 22, 55, 57, 59, 85
soprano, 33
sound, 18, 21–23, 55, 58
stage manager, 18, 20–21, 57
stage fright, 17, 70
strike, 59
summer stock, 71, **71**, 76
swing, 79

table read, 49–50
tenor, 33–34
"Ten-Second Rule," 30–31
Tony Award, 53, 70, 75, 79, 83
traditional musicals, 37
triple threat, 13, 66–67

vocal coach, 7–9, **9**, 17, 40, 69, 86
vocal range, 8, 10, 29, 32–34

warming up, 6, 40–41, 50–51, 69
West Side Story, 4, 5, 27, 34–35, 46, 49, 53
Wicked, 27, 36–37, 61

Zuckerberg, Randi, 82–83, **82**

ABOUT THE AUTHOR

Ruth Bjorklund lives on Bainbridge Island, Washington. The author of numerous books, she has a master's degree in library and information science from the University of Washington. A versatile author, she has written a book on costume design for this series, as well as books on subjects as diverse as endangered animals, United States history, alternative fuels, immigration, contemporary biography, world cultures, and recently the internment of Japanese Americans during World War II.